Listen, My Children

POEMS FOR FOURTH GRADERS

A CORE KNOWLEDGE® BOOK

LISTEN, MY CHILDREN: POEMS FOR FOURTH GRADERS
ONE IN A SERIES, *POEMS FOR KINDERGARTNERS—FIFTH GRADERS*,
COLLECTING THE POEMS IN THE *CORE KNOWLEDGE SEQUENCE*

A CORE KNOWLEDGE® BOOK

SERIES EDITOR: SUSAN TYLER HITCHCOCK
RESEARCHER: JEANNE NICHOLSON SILER
EDITORIAL ASSISTANT: KRISTEN D. MOSES
CONSULTANT: STEPHEN B. CUSHMAN
GENERAL EDITOR: E. D. HIRSCH JR.

LIBRARY OF CONGRESS CARD CATALOG NUMBER: 00-111615
ISBN 1-890517-32-1

PRINTED IN CANADA
DESIGN BY DIANE NELSON GRAPHIC DESIGN
COVER ART COPYRIGHT © BY LANCE HIDY, LANCE@LANCEHIDY.COM

CORE KNOWLEDGE FOUNDATION
801 EAST HIGH STREET
CHARLOTTESVILLE, VIRGINIA 22902
WWW.COREKNOWLEDGE.ORG

About this Book

"LISTEN, MY CHILDREN, and you shall hear . . ." So begins a famous poem about Paul Revere, written by Henry Wadsworth Longfellow in 1855. This opening line reminds us that every time we read a poem, we hear that poem as well. The sounds and rhythms of the words are part of the poem's meaning. Poems are best understood when read out loud, or when a reader hears the sounds of the words in his or her head while reading silently.

This six-volume series collects all the poems in the Core Knowledge Sequence for kindergarten through fifth grade. Each volume includes occasional notes about the poems and biographical sketches about the poems' authors, but the focus is really the poems themselves. Some have been chosen because they reflect times past; others because of their literary fame; still others were selected because they express states of mind shared by many children.

This selection of poetry, part of the *Core Knowledge Sequence*, is based on the work of E. D. Hirsch Jr., author of *Cultural Literacy* and *The Schools We Need*. The Sequence outlines a core curriculum for preschool through grade eight in English and language arts, history and geography, math, science, art, and music. It is designed to ensure that children are exposed to the essential knowledge that establishes cultural literacy as they also acquire a broad, firm foundation for higher-level schooling. Its first version was developed in 1990 at a convention of teachers and subject matter experts. Revised in 1995 to reflect the classroom experience of Core Knowledge teachers, the Sequence is now used in hundreds of schools across America. Its content also guides the Core Knowledge Series, *What Your Kindergartner—Sixth Grader Needs to Know.*

Contents

Monday's Child Is Fair of Face

Author unknown

Monday's child is fair of face,
Tuesday's child is full of grace,
Wednesday's child is full of woe,
Thursday's child has far to go,
Friday's child is loving and giving,
Saturday's child works hard for a living,
But the child that is born on the Sabbath day
Is fair and wise and good and gay.

Afternoon on a Hill

by Edna St. Vincent Millay

I will be the gladdest thing
    Under the sun!
I will touch a hundred flowers
    And pick not one.

I will look at cliffs and clouds
    With quiet eyes,
Watch the wind bow down the grass,
    And the grass rise.

And when lights begin to show,
    Up from the town,
I will mark which must be mine,
    And then start down.

Clouds

by Christina G. Rossetti

White sheep, white sheep
On a blue hill,
When the wind stops
You all stand still.
When the wind blows,
You walk away slow.
White sheep, white sheep,
Where do you go?

Things
by Eloise Greenfield

Went to the corner
Walked in the store
Bought me some candy
Ain't got it no more
Ain't got it no more

Went to the beach
Played on the shore
Built me a sandhouse
Ain't got it no more
Ain't got it no more

Went to the kitchen
Lay down on the floor
Made me a poem
Still got it
Still got it

Fog
by *Carl Sandburg*

The fog comes
on little cat feet.

It sits looking
over harbor and city
on silent haunches
and then moves on.

Carl Sandburg
1878–1967

The child of Swedish immigrants, Carl Sandburg
came to be known for poems about America,
written in plain language so many people could
understand them. Sandburg's family was so poor, he
had to leave school at the age of 13 to earn money.
He fought in the Spanish-American War. He wrote
newspaper articles for a living until his poetry began
receiving attention. He also collected American folk
songs and ballads.

the drum

by Nikki Giovanni

daddy says the world is
a drum tight and hard
and i told him
i'm gonna beat
out my own rhythm

Dreams
by Langston Hughes

Hold fast to dreams
For if dreams die
Life is a broken-winged bird
That cannot fly.

Hold fast to dreams
For when dreams go
Life is a barren field
Frozen with snow.

Langston Hughes
1902–1967

Langston Hughes was considered the most important poet of the "Harlem Renaissance," when African-American musicians, dancers, writers, and performers living in New York City in the 1920s worked together to create great works of art. Hughes was born in Joplin, Missouri. After he had published his first book of poems, called *The Weary Blues,* he was admitted to Lincoln University in Pennsylvania. He lived in Mexico and France as well as in New York City. Many of his poems reflect the ways African Americans lived and talked in the city in the first half of the 20th century.

The Rhinoceros
by Ogden Nash

The rhino is a homely beast,
For human eyes he's not a feast.
But you and I will never know
Why Nature chose to make him so.
Farewell, farewell, you old rhinoceros,
I'll stare at something less prepoceros.

Clarence

by Shel Silverstein

Clarence Lee from Tennessee
Loved the commercials he saw on TV.
He watched with wide believing eyes
And bought everything they advertised —
Cream to make his skin feel better,
Spray to make his hair look wetter,
Bleach to make his white things whiter,
Stylish jeans that fit much tighter.
Toothpaste for his cavities,
Powder for his doggie's fleas,
Purple mouthwash for his breath,
Deodorant to stop his sweat.
He bought each cereal they presented,
Bought each game that they invented.
Then one day he looked and saw
"A brand-new Maw, a better Paw!
New, improved in every way —
Hurry, order yours today!"
So, of course, our little Clarence
Sent off for two brand-new parents.
The new ones came in the morning mail,
The old ones he sold at a garage sale.
And now they all are doing fine:
His new folks treat him sweet and kind,
His old ones work in an old coal mine.
So if your Maw and Paw are mean
And make you eat your lima beans
And make you wash and make you wait
And never let you stay up late
And scream and scold and preach and pout,
That simply means they're wearing out.
So send off for two brand-new parents
And you'll be as happy as little Clarence.

Humanity

by Elma Stuckey

If I am blind and need someone
To keep me safe from harm,
It matters not the race to me
Of the one who takes my arm.

If I am saved from drowning
As I grasp and grope,
I will not stop to see the face
Of the one who throws the rope.

Or if out on some battlefield
I'm falling faint and weak,
The one who gently lifts me up
May any language speak.

We sip the water clear and cool,
No matter the hand that gives it.
A life that's lived worthwhile and fine,
What matters the one who lives it?

A Tragic Story

by William Makepeace Thackeray

There lived a sage in days of yore,
And he a handsome pigtail wore:
But wondered much, and sorrowed more,
    Because it hung behind him.

He mused upon this curious case,
And swore he'd change the pigtail's place,
And have it hanging at his face,
    Not dangling there behind him.

Says he, "The mystery I've found —
I'll turn me round," — he turned him round;
    but still it hung behind him.

Then round, and round, and out and in,
All day the puzzled sage did spin;
In vain — it mattered not a pin —
    The pigtail hung behind him.

And right and left, and round about,
And up and down, and in and out
He turned; but still the pigtail stout
    Hung steadily behind him.

And though his efforts never slack,
And though he twist, and twirl, and tack,
Alas! Still faithful to his back,
    The pigtail hangs behind him.

Henry Wadsworth Longfellow
1807–1882

Henry Wadsworth Longfellow was a well-loved
American poet of the 19th century. His poems still
shape our ideas about some of the great stories and
characters of American history — like Paul Revere,
for example.

Paul Revere's Ride

by Henry Wadsworth Longfellow

Listen, my children, and you shall hear
Of the midnight ride of Paul Revere,
On the eighteenth of April, in Seventy-five;
Hardly a man is now alive
Who remembers that famous day and year.

He said to his friend, "If the British march
By land or sea from the town tonight,
Hang a lantern aloft in the belfry arch
Of the North Church tower as a signal light —
One, if by land, and two, if by sea;
And I on the opposite shore shall be.
Ready to ride and spread the alarm
Through every Middlesex village and farm,
For the country folk to be up and to arm."

BELFRY [BELL-free] Bell tower.

Then he said "Good night!" and with muffled oar
Silently rowed to the Charlestown shore,
Just as the moon rose over the bay,
Where swinging wide at her moorings lay
The *Somerset*, British man-of-war;
A phantom ship, with each mast and spar
Across the moon like a prison bar,
And a huge black hulk, that was magnified
By its own reflection in the tide.

MAN-OF-WAR A Navy warship.

MAST, SPAR The vertical and horizontal poles to which sails attach.

Meanwhile, his friend, through alley and street,
Wanders and watches with eager ears,
Till in the silence around him he hears
The muster of men at the barrack door,
And the measured tread of the grenadiers,
Marching down to their boats on the shore.

MUSTER Roll call.

GRENADIERS [gren-ah-DEERS] Soldiers armed with grenades.

Then he climbed the tower of the Old North Church,
By wooden stairs, with steady tread,
To the belfry-chamber overhead,
And startled the pigeons from their perch
On the somber rafters, that round him made
Masses and moving shapes of shade —
By trembling ladder, steep and tall
To the highest window in the wall,
Where he paused to listen and look down
A moment on the roof of the town,
And the moonlight flowing over all.

Beneath in the churchyard, lay the dead,
In their night-encampment on the hill,
Wrapped in silence so deep and still
That he could hear, like a sentinel's tread,
The watchful night-wind, as it went
Creeping along from tent to tent,
And seeming to whisper, "All is well!"
A moment only he feels the spell
Of the place and the hour and the secret dread
Of the lonely belfry and the dead;
For suddenly all his thoughts are bent
On a shadowy something far away,
Where the river widens to meet the bay —
A line of black that bends and floats
On the rising tide, like a bridge of boats.

SENTINEL A soldier standing guard.

Paul Revere was a silversmith in Boston during the time of the American Revolution. Thanks to Longfellow's poem, he is remembered as the American patriot who rode through the night to warn that the British were coming. Longfellow used "poetic license" — a phrase meaning a writer has changed facts to make a better story. He wrote about Paul Revere, never mentioning William Dawes and Samuel Prescott, the other two men who spread the alarm with Revere.

Meanwhile, impatient to mount and ride,
Booted and spurred, with a heavy stride
On the opposite shore walked Paul Revere.
Now he patted his horse's side,
Now he gazed at the landscape far and near,
Then, impetuous, stamped the earth,
And turned and tightened his saddle girth;
But mostly he watched with eager search
The belfry tower of the Old North Church,
As it rose above the graves on the hill.
Lonely and spectral and somber and still.

And lo! as he looks, on the belfry's height
A glimmer, and then a gleam of light!
He springs to his saddle, the bridle he turns,
But lingers and gazes, till full on his sight
A second lamp in the belfry burns!

IMPETUOUS
Sudden and forceful.

SPECTRAL
Spooky and ghostlike.

A hurry of hoofs in a village street,
A shape in the moonlight, a bulk in the dark,
And beneath, from the pebbles, in passing, a spark
Struck out by a steed flying fearless and fleet:
That was all! And yet, through the gloom and the light,
The fate of a nation was riding that night;
And the spark struck out by the steed, in his flight,
Kindled the land into flame with its heat.

STEED
Horse.

He has left the village and mounted the steep,
And beneath him, tranquil and broad and deep,
Is the Mystic, meeting the ocean tides;
And under the alders that skirt its edge,
Now soft on the sand, now loud on the ledge,
Is heard the tramp of his steed as he rides.

THE MYSTIC
A river that
flows through
Boston into the
Atlantic
Ocean.

It was twelve by the village clock,
When he crossed the bridge into Medford town.
He heard the crowing of the cock,
And the barking of the farmer's dog,
And felt the damp of the river fog,
That rises after the sun goes down.
It was one by the village clock,
When he galloped into Lexington.
He saw the gilded weathercock
Swim in the moonlight as he passed,
And the meeting-house windows, blank and bare,
Gaze at him with a spectral glare,
As if they already stood aghast
At the bloody work they would look upon.

**GILDED
WEATHERCOCK**
Gold
weathervane.

It was two by the village clock,
When he came to the bridge in Concord Town.
He heard the bleating of the flock,
And the twitter of birds among the trees,
And felt the breath of the morning breeze
Blowing over the meadows brown.
And one was safe and asleep in his bed
Who at the bridge would be first to fall,
Who that day would be lying dead,
Pierced by a British musket-ball.

You know the rest. In the books you have read
How the British Regulars fired and fled —
How the farmers gave them ball for ball,
From behind each fence and farmyard wall,
Chasing the red-coats down the lane,
Then crossing the fields to emerge again
Under the trees at the turn of the road,
And only pausing to fire and load.

BRITISH REGULARS Professional British soldiers who fought during the Revolution.

So through the night rode Paul Revere;
And so through the night went his cry of alarm
To every Middlesex village and farm —
A cry of defiance and not of fear,
A voice in the darkness, a knock at the door,
And a word that shall echo for evermore!
For, borne on the night-wind of the Past,
Through all our history, to the last,
In the hour of darkness and peril and need,
The people will awaken and listen to hear
The hurrying hoof-beats of that steed,
And the midnight message of Paul Revere.

George Washington

by Rosemary Benét and Stephen Vincent Benét

Sing hey! for bold George Washington,
That jolly British tar,
King George's famous admiral
From Hull to Zanzibar!
No – wait a minute – something's wrong –
George *wished* to sail the foam.
But, when his mother thought, aghast,
Of Georgie shinning up a mast,
Her tears and protests flowed so fast
That George remained at home.

Sing ho! for grave Washington,
The staid Virginia squire,
Who farms his fields and hunts his hounds
And aims at nothing higher!
Stop, stop, it's going wrong again!
George *liked* to live on farms,
But, when the Colonies agreed
They could and should and would be freed,
They called on George to do the deed
And George cried, "Shoulder arms!"

Sing ha! for Emperor Washington,
That hero of renown,
Who freed his land from Britain's rule
To win a golden crown!
No, no, that's what George *might* have won
But didn't, for he said,
"There's not much point about a king,
They're pretty but they're apt to sting
And, as for crowns — the heavy thing
Would only hurt my head."

Sing ho! for our George Washington!
(At last I've got it straight.)
The first in war, the first in peace,
The goodly and the great.
But, when you think about him now,
From here to Valley Forge,
Remember this — he might have been
A highly different specimen,
And, where on earth would we be, then?
I'm glad that George was George.

Ralph Waldo Emerson
1803–1882

Ralph Waldo Emerson considered himself a poet, but his speeches and essays were also important. He influenced many American writers, including Henry David Thoreau, who wrote *Walden*; Nathaniel Hawthorne, who wrote *The Scarlet Letter*; and Herman Melville, who wrote *Moby-Dick*. Emerson was a leader of the "transcendentalists." Transcendentalists believed they would find truth in the human spirit and in nature rather than in the church.

Concord Hymn

by Ralph Waldo Emerson

By the rude bridge that arched the flood,
    Their flag to April's breeze unfurled,
Here once the embattled farmers stood
    And fired the shot heard round the world.

The foe long since in silence slept;
    Alike the conqueror silent sleeps;
And Time the ruined bridge has swept
    Down the dark stream which seaward creeps.

On this green bank, by this soft stream,
    We set to-day a votive stone;
That memory may their deed redeem,
    When, like our sires, our sons are gone.

VOTIVE STONE
A memorial stone.

Spirit, that made those heroes dare
    To die, and leave their children free,
Bid Time and Nature gently spare
    The shaft we raise to them and thee.

SHAFT
A tall, straight object; here, a monument.

Emerson wrote this poem for a ceremony in Concord, Massachusetts, when a monument in honor of the minutemen of the Revolutionary War was unveiled. The "shot heard round the world" has become a well-known saying. The phrase is Emerson's way of suggesting that when the American Revolution began, people all over the world paid attention to the new ideas of democracy and independence for which Americans were fighting.

The Pobble Who Has No Toes

by Edward Lear

The Pobble who has no toes,
　　Had once as many as we;
When they said, "Some day you may lose them all;"
　　He replied "Fish Fiddle de-dee!"
And his Aunt Jobiska made him drink,
Lavender water tinged with pink;
For she said, "The World in general knows
There's nothing so good for a Pobble's Toes!"

The Pobble who has no toes,
　　Swam across the Bristol Channel;
But before he set out he wrapped his nose
　　In a piece of scarlet flannel.
For his Aunt Jobiska said, "No harm
Can come to his toes if his nose is warm;
And it's perfectly known that a Pobble's toes
Are safe — provided he minds his nose."

The Pobble swam fast and well.
　　And when boats or ships came near him
He tinkledy-binkledy-winkled a bell
　　So that all the world could hear him.
And all the Sailors and Admirals cried,
When they saw him nearing the further side —
"He has gone to fish, for his Aunt Jobiska's
Runcible Cat with crimson whiskers!"

But before he touched the shore —
　　The shore of the Bristol Channel
A sea-green Porpoise carried away
　　His wrapper of scarlet flannel.

BRISTOL CHANNEL
The body of water between England and Wales.

And when he came to observe his feet
Formerly garnished with toes so neat
His face at once became forlorn
On perceiving that all his toes were gone!

And nobody knew
    From that dark day to the present,
Whoso had taken the Pobble's toes,
    In a manner so far from pleasant.
Whether the shrimps or crawfish gray,
Or crafty Mermaids stole them away —
Nobody knew; and nobody knows
How the Pobble was robbed of his twice five toes!

The Pobble who has no toes
    Was placed in a friendly Bark,
And they rowed him back, and carried him up,
    To his Aunt Jobiska's Park.
And she made him a feast at his earnest wish
Of eggs and buttercups fried with fish;
And he said, "It's a fact the whole world knows,
That Pobbles are happier without their toes."

BARK
A small boat.

What on earth is a "Runcible Cat"? "Runcible" is a nonsense word that Edward Lear made up. He also used it in his poem, "The Owl and the Pussycat," to describe a spoon. Since then, the word has entered the English language, and nowadays people call a spoon with fork-like prongs a "runcible spoon." But that doesn't explain what a "Runcible Cat" is, does it? You decide.

Life Doesn't Frighten Me

by Maya Angelou

Shadows on the wall
Noises down the hall
Life doesn't frighten me at all
Bad dogs barking loud
Big ghosts in a cloud
Life doesn't frighten me at all.

Mean old Mother Goose
Lions on the loose
They don't frighten me at all
Dragons breathing flame
On my counterpane
That doesn't frighten me at all.

I go boo
Make them shoo
I make fun
Way they run
I won't cry
So they fly
I just smile
They go wild
Life doesn't frighten me at all.

Tough guys in a fight
All alone at night
Life doesn't frighten me at all.
Panthers in the park
Strangers in the dark
No, they don't frighten me at all.

That new classroom where
Boys all pull my hair
(Kissy little girls
With their hair in curls)
They don't frighten me at all.

Don't show me frogs and snakes
And listen for my scream,
If I'm afraid at all
It's only in my dreams.

I've got a magic charm
That I keep up my sleeve,
I can walk the ocean floor
And never have to breathe.

Life doesn't frighten me at all
Not at all
Not at all.
Life doesn't frighten me at all.

Maya Angelou
1928–

Maya Angelou is an author and teacher, actress and activist. She has worked with civil rights leaders, including Martin Luther King Jr., and with government leaders, including Presidents Ford and Carter. In 1993 she recited her poem "On the Pulse of Morning" at President Clinton's inauguration. The first volume of her autobiography, *I Know Why the Caged Bird Sings,* tells about growing up in the United States in the 1930s, when black and white children attended different schools.

Acknowledgments

Every care has been taken to trace and acknowledge copyright of the poems and images in this volume. If accidental infringement has occurred, the editor offers apologies and welcomes communications that allow proper acknowledgment in subsequent editions.

"**Things**" from *Honey, I Love,* by Eloise Greenfield. Copyright © 1978 by Eloise Greenfield. Used by permission of HarperCollins Publishers.

"**Fog**" from *Chicago Poems* by Carl Sandburg. Copyright © 1916 by Holt, Rinehart and Winston, renewed 1944 by Carl Sandburg. Reprinted by permission of Harcourt, Inc.

"**the drum**" from *Spin a Soft Black Song* by Nikki Giovanni. Copyright ©1971,1985 by Nikki Giovanni. Reprinted by permission of Hill and Wang, a division of Farrar, Straus and Giroux, LLC.

"**Dreams**" from *Collected Poems* by Langston Hughes. Copyright © 1994 by the Estate of Langston Hughes. Reprinted by permission of Alfred A. Knopf, a Division of Random House, Inc.

"**The Rhinoceros**" from *Verses from 1929 On* by Ogden Nash. Copyright © 1933 by Ogden Nash, renewed. Reprinted by permission of Curtis Brown, Ltd.

"**Clarence**" from *A Light in the Attic,* by Shel Silverstein. Copyright © 1981 by Evil Eye Music, Inc. Selection reprinted by permission of HarperCollins Publishers.

"**Humanity**" from *The Collected Poems of Elma Stuckey* by Elma Stuckey. Copyright © 1988; all rights reserved. Reprinted by permission of Transaction Publishers.

"**George Washington**" from *A Book of Americans,* by Rosemary and Stephen Vincent Benet, Holt, Rinehart and Winston. Copyright © 1933 by Rosemary and Stephen Vincent Benet, copyright renewed © 1961 by Rosemary Carr Benet, reprinted with permission of Brandt & Brandt Literary Agents, Ltd.

"**Life Doesn't Frighten Me**" from *And Still I Rise* by Maya Angelou. Copyright © 1978 by Maya Angelou. Reprinted by permission of Random House, Inc.

Images:
Carl Sandburg: © Bettmann/CORBIS
Langston Hughes: © CORBIS
Ralph Waldo Emerson: By permission of the Clifton Waller Barrett Library of American Literature, Special Collections Department, University of Virginia Library
Henry Wadsworth Longfellow: © CORBIS
Maya Angelou: © Bettmann/CORBIS